MERLIN AND TH... ...OR OB

Imagine going on a geography field trip to look at rock formations and bumping into Merlin the magician in a cave! That's just what happens to Becky and Daniel and they ask Merlin to give them a crash course in geography. He takes them on a whirlwind trip around the world, exploring lots of fascinating facts and features of the planet Earth. But Merlin also sets them a task – to find a place called Ob. To do this they have to solve 39 puzzles. Each time a puzzle is solved a section of the World Map at the beginning of the book is shaded in. Only one section should remain and in that section (but it has to be the right section!) Ob will be found.

Now you can join Becky, Daniel and Merlin and help them in their quest for Ob. On the way you'll learn many things about the earth and the people and creatures who inhabit it. You'll also have fun solving all the puzzles!

A Puffin Geography Adventure Puzzle Book.

A Puffin History Adventure Puzzle Book

MERLIN AND THE SEARCH FOR ROMAN BRITAIN

CLIVE BROWN

MERLIN

AND THE SEARCH FOR

OB

ILLUSTRATED BY
DAVID WOODWARD

PUFFIN BOOKS

PUFFIN BOOKS

Published by the Penguin Group
Penguin Books Ltd, 27 Wrights Lane, London W8 5TZ, England
Penguin Books USA Inc., 375 Hudson Street, New York, New York 10014, USA
Penguin Books Australia Ltd, Ringwood, Victoria, Australia
Penguin Books Canada Ltd, 10 Alcorn Avenue, Toronto, Ontario, Canada M4V 3B2
Penguin Books (NZ) Ltd, 182–190 Wairau Road, Auckland 10, New Zealand

Penguin Books Ltd, Registered Offices: Harmondsworth, Middlesex, England

Published in Puffin Books 1993
10 9 8 7 6 5 4 3 2 1

Text copyright © Complete Editions, 1993
Illustrations copyright © David Woodward, 1993
All rights reserved

The moral right of the author has been asserted

Typeset by Datix International Limited, Bungay, Suffolk
Filmset in Monophoto Helvetica
Printed in Great Britain by Clays Ltd, St Ives plc

Introduction

The Search for Ob will take you on an exciting adventure around the world, exploring lots of fascinating facts and features of our planet. Your aim, as you travel through the book with Merlin, Becky and Daniel, is to find Ob.

In the next part of this book you can read the story of how the three travellers met and began their journey. You will also see a map of the world divided into forty sections. As you travel through the book, you'll find thirty-nine puzzles to solve. Each puzzle is accompanied by a box like this, offering you a number of possible answers.

If you choose ...	Turn to the world map and cross out ...
A	13
B	9
C	27

If you think the correct answer to the puzzle is *A*, then take a pencil, go back to the map of the world, and cross off square 13. Then go on to the next puzzle and try to solve that.

If you answer all thirty-nine puzzles correctly, you should be left with only one section of the map that hasn't been crossed off. This is the square where Ob is located.

If you get some of the puzzles wrong, you'll be left with some sections that have been crossed off more than once, and others that haven't been crossed off at all! If that happens, try the puzzles again and see if you get different answers. The more accurate you are, the easier it will be to find Ob.

When you're left with only one square on the map, or you've narrowed the choice down as far as you can, you're well on your way to finding Ob. All you have to do now is turn to page 95, where you'll find some more clues that will enable you to work out precisely where Ob is.

If you get really stuck and there's no way you can work out the answer, you'll find the solution on pages 101–105. But only use it as a last resort!

Merlin and the Search for Ob

'Everybody out of the bus!' called Mr Harrison, the geography teacher. 'And don't forget to bring your clipboards and information sheets.'

Becky and Daniel, who'd been sitting at the back, were the last ones to climb down. Dark clouds loomed over the cliffs. The hills in the distance looked black and gloomy.

Becky felt pretty gloomy herself. 'I don't like the seaside when the sun's not shining,' she told Daniel. They'd both been looking forward to the geography field trip, but neither of them was enjoying it much. They kept getting wet and muddy.

Daniel buttoned up his parka. It was chilly in the wind. 'I can't see the point of bringing us to the beach when it's too cold to go swimming,' he said.

'Line up in pairs,' Mr Harrison instructed in his cheerful way. 'We're going to walk down to the beach so that we can study the rock formations.'

Becky raised her eyebrows. 'Rock formations? What do we want to look at rocks for?'

The class set off, walking behind Mr Harrison. There were steps leading down from the car park to the beach below and they all climbed down. 'Follow me!' ordered Mr Harrison when they'd reached the sand safely. 'And just take a look at the sedimentary layers in the cliffs as we go. Keep a lookout for fault lines.'

'I don't know what he's on about,' said Daniel, watching their teacher striding off down the beach. 'What's so interesting about rocks?' But he and Becky went on, following the other children.

A hundred metres along the beach, Becky spotted the entrance to a cave. She turned excitedly to Daniel. 'Why don't we go and explore in there while the others go looking at rocks?' she whispered.

Daniel glanced round. Mr Harrison was up ahead, with most of the children grouped round him as he pointed to something in the cliff. The other teachers and helpers were gazing at the spot to which he was pointing.

'Quick!' giggled Daniel, and he and Becky scampered across the sand and slipped inside the cave.

It was dim and echoey inside. Rocks and bits of driftwood littered the sandy floor. 'I bet there's a treasure chest buried somewhere in here,' said Daniel confidently, scuffing up the sand around a particularly big rock.

'Then let's find it!' exclaimed Becky. *Find it, find it, find it . . .* her voice echoed back from the walls around.

'If there's an echo in here, the cave must go back a long way,' Daniel said. 'Let's explore.'

The cave went back a few metres but no more. 'This must be the end of it,' said Daniel, disappointed. From the sound of the echo, he'd thought it would be larger. And there was no treasure. They looked everywhere, but there wasn't a single gold coin or diamond necklace in sight. Just an empty crisps packet and a plastic bottle. Becky unscrewed the bottle cap.

4

'There might be a genie inside who'll grant us three wishes,' she said hopefully. But the bottle was empty too.

The pair of them sat forlornly on a rock just inside the cave's entrance. 'Let's wait till the others come back. We can tag along and they'll never notice we were gone,' suggested Daniel.

'OK.' Becky flipped through the information sheets and questionnaires that Mr Harrison had given them to read and complete during the field trip. 'Have you seen all this?' she groaned. 'It's all about rock formations and coastlines and maps. And I don't know a single answer to the questions. What are we going to do?'

Daniel shrugged. He looked equally fed up. 'I don't care what Mr Harrison says, geography's the most boring subject in the world.'

Becky giggled. 'We said that once before, about history. Remember? And it turned out not to be boring at all!'

'Yeah, I remember,' nodded Daniel. 'But that was only because Merlin took us back in time to Roman Britain. He's not here now.'

'Maybe we should call him,' suggested Becky. 'If he's passing on a time warp, he might hear us and come and help.'

Daniel sighed. 'He's probably jousting with King Arthur and the Knights of the Round Table, or playing tennis with Henry VIII.'

'It's worth a try, anyway,' decided Becky. And she yelled at the top of her voice, 'Merlin! Merlin! Come and help us! We need you!'

Daniel joined in and they tried again. But nothing happened. Not a sausage. 'It looks as if we've got to

learn about geography on our own,' concluded Daniel.

'Hold on.' Becky pointed to the corner of the cave, where there was just the faintest green glow. A curl of green smoke rose to the roof. 'Something's happening,' she murmured.

And then suddenly there was a bang and a green flash, and Merlin appeared, looking flustered. In one hand he held a big white napkin.

'Where's the emergency?' he spluttered, looking round the cave.

'Merlin!' Daniel and Becky raced up to him and buried their faces in his long robe. It smelt of green smoke and peppermints, just as it always did.

'Are we pleased to see you!' grinned Becky.

But Merlin wasn't looking very pleased. 'When I heard you calling I thought there was an emergency. I was right in the middle of having dinner with Cleopatra. The most delicious roast dormice I've ever eaten.' He frowned. 'You appear to have called me out to a cave in the middle of nowhere – and all for nothing!'

'It's not nothing, Merlin,' explained Daniel. 'We're on a geography field trip.'

'And we hate geography,' added Becky, 'and it keeps raining.'

'And we've got to fill in all these questionnaires.' Daniel waved them at him. 'And we don't know a *thing*.'

'And I suppose you want *me* to give you a crash course in geography?' Merlin stroked his moustache. He still looked cross.

'Yes, please,' said Becky coaxingly. 'You're the only person we know who can make it interesting.'

'Mr Harrison just talks about boring old rocks,' added Daniel.

'But rocks are fascinating!' protested Mer[...]
can learn so much from a good rock.'

The children's faces fell. 'You don't belie[...]
asked Merlin. They shook their heads.

'In that case,' said Merlin, 'I'd better prove it to

you. Geography's one of my favourite subjects. I don't like to hear people say it's boring.'

'You'll take us on a tour of the world and teach us all we need to know?' Becky exclaimed.

'All right,' nodded Merlin. 'I was due to meet Christopher Columbus for tea, but he can get on with discovering the world without me. But –' he wagged one long, wizardy finger with a green sparkling ring at them, '– I'm not going to do all the work. I'm setting you a challenge and it's up to you to solve it.'

'What's the challenge?' asked Daniel.

Merlin thought for a minute, then, 'I want you to find Ob,' he said.

Daniel and Becky stared at each other. 'Who's Ob?' Daniel asked.

'Or what?' Becky looked mystified, but Merlin just smiled.

'That', he said firmly, 'is for you to find out. For every puzzle you solve correctly as we go round the world, you'll get a clue. If you put all the clues together, and you listen carefully to what I tell you, you'll find Ob.'

'All right.' Becky and Daniel nodded. 'Where shall we start?'

Merlin glanced at the time warp watch he wore on his wrist. 'I think we'll start at the very beginning,' he said. 'And we're in luck! Here comes a time warp that will take us back 4,600 million years . . .'

And before Becky or Daniel could even look surprised, there was a bang and a flash of green smoke, and they were off on their adventure . . .

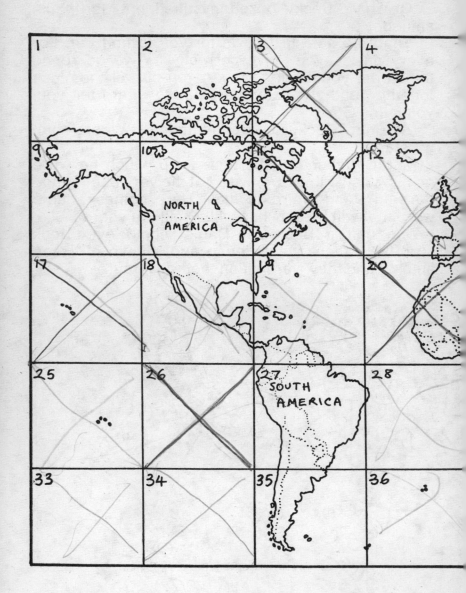

1	2	3	4
9	10 NORTH	11	12
17	18 AMERICA	19	20
25	26	27 SOUTH	28
33	34	35 AMERICA	36

NORTH
AMERICA

SOUTH
AMERICA

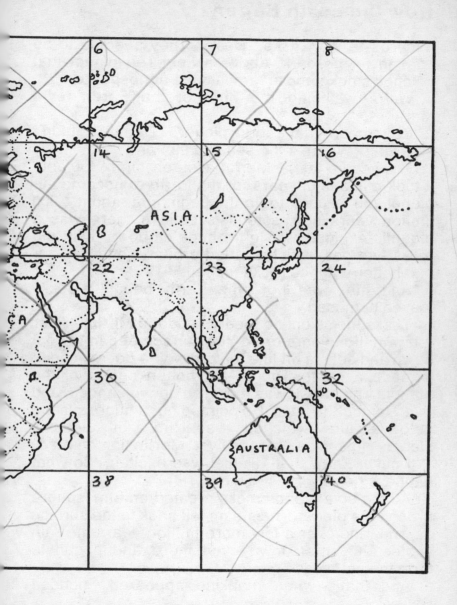

How the Earth Began

'Where are we?' asked Becky. They seemed to be floating in the dark, above a fiery red planet that belched smoke and steam into the atmosphere.

'We're watching the birth of the Earth,' said Merlin.

'You mean that's our planet?' Daniel couldn't believe it. 'Where's the sea and the land?'

'They come later,' Merlin assured him. 'You see, it took millions of years for the Earth to become the planet you're used to. In the beginning, about 4,600 million years ago, scientists believe there was a gigantic explosion. It left a huge cloud of dust and rocks and gas, which swirled around getting hotter and hotter until the rocks melted.'

'And that was how the Earth began?' Becky looked bemused.

'That's the scientific theory,' nodded Merlin. 'After a few million years or so, the surface began to cool down and set – a bit like the gravy you get at school. It made a crust around the molten centre of the planet. The crust was covered in volcanoes and rivers of molten lava.' He pointed out a huge volcano below; as they watched, it sent up a big cloud of steam. 'Not a nice place to live,' Merlin commented.

'I never knew that!' Daniel was excited. 'So what happens next?'

'All the steam and smoke created an atmosphere around the planet. The steam fell back to the surface as rain, and over a few more million years the rain cooled the crust down even more and began to form the first seas.'

'And that's when mankind appeared,' nodded Becky.

14

Merlin held up his finger, the one with the shiny green ring. 'You're jumping the gun a bit, young lady. Before we get to human beings, I think we'll have a puzzle.'

Earth Birth Puzzle
Here's a diagram showing the Earth as it was several million years ago. As you'll see, there are arrows pointing to several features. Put the names listed below in the correct boxes. Which word is in the shaded box?

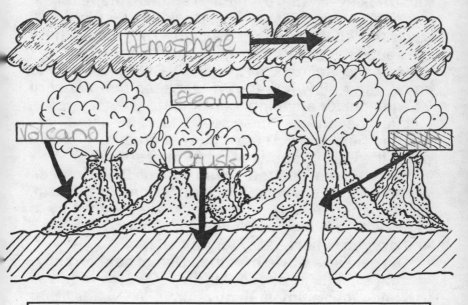

If you choose . . .	Turn to the world map and cross out . . .
Steam	40
Volcano	35
Crust	30
Lava	26
Atmosphere	3

Hello, Humans!

'Right,' said Merlin, wafting away the cloud of green smoke that had enveloped them. 'We've now jumped forward in time. It's only about a million years before you went on your geography field trip.'

'Is that all?' giggled Daniel. What was a million years, when the Earth was so old?

Becky and Daniel gazed around. The volcanoes had gone. Now there were plants beneath their feet and trees everywhere – though some of them looked strange in comparison with the kind of plants and trees the children were used to. They could hear the sounds of animals and birds in the forest.

'How did animals begin life?' Becky wanted to know. After all, when they'd last seen the planet, it was too hot for anything to live on it.

'Life began in the sea,' Merlin explained. 'Remember I told you how the rain gradually cooled down the Earth's surface and formed seas?'

The children nodded. 'Well, about 2,000 million years after the explosion that formed the Earth, plants began to grow in the seas. They were tiny to begin with, but they produced a gas called oxygen – and oxygen is necessary for animal life.'

'Oxygen is what we breathe,' Daniel said proudly.

'That's right,' nodded Merlin. 'Oxygen allowed fish and other animals to develop in the water. After another 2,000 million years of evolution, some of these creatures crawled out of the sea and began living on land.'

'Our ancestors!' breathed Becky.

'Not quite,' laughed Merlin. 'These things happen very, very slowly. But about 15 million years ago, apes began to evolve. They are the animal "family"

16

from which humans are descended. But it wasn't until about one million years ago that these creatures became recognizably human.'

'Can we see some now?' demanded Daniel impatiently.

'There's a family living just over there,' said Merlin. 'I think they'll make an excellent puzzle for you.'

Human Puzzle
Here are two pictures of some of the first humans. How many differences can you spot between the two pictures?

If you choose . . .	Turn to the world map and cross out . . .
12 differences	20
7 differences	25
4 differences	2

A Floating Jigsaw

'Now let's go back in time again so that I can show you something else,' said Merlin. '200 million years should be enough.' There was a flash and a bang and the children closed their eyes.

'We're back in space!' exclaimed Becky when the green smoke had cleared.

'That's right. We're here because I want you to look down at the Earth from a distance,' Merlin explained. Below them the planet sparkled blue and green, just as they'd seen it in pictures. But there was something strange about it.

'All the land's joined together in one big lump!' squeaked Daniel.

'Well spotted,' smiled Merlin. 'Now, remember, the middle of the Earth is made of hot, liquid rock.'

'With a crust over the top,' Becky reminded him.

'Exactly,' agreed Merlin. 'The crust is about 60 kilometres deep in most places. Originally, all the land sticking up above the sea formed one big mass – as you can see.'

'So what happened?' the children asked.

'Very, very slowly, the Earth's crust began to crack into separate pieces,' Merlin told them. 'These pieces are called plates. They're like the bits of a giant jigsaw puzzle.'

The children looked impressed. 'I never knew that,' breathed Becky.

'That's not all,' said Merlin. 'Gradually, over millions of years, these plates drifted away from each other to form the picture of the world we're used to in the twentieth century. But the world won't stay that way. The plates are still moving. In a few million years, the world could look totally different!'

'Amazing!' breathed Becky and Daniel.

'Yes,' nodded Merlin. 'So while we're on the subject of plates, let's have a puzzle.'

Jigsaw Puzzle
Here are two maps. The first one shows the world as it is now. The second shows how the scientists think all the continents might have been joined together 200 million years ago. One area of the old map has been shaded in. What is it now called?

If you choose . . .	*Turn to the world map and cross out . . .*
North America	7
Africa	19
South America	11
Europe	27

Let's Rock!

'Now,' said Merlin, when the three time travellers were safely back on Earth again, 'let's talk rocks.'

'Not rocks!' Becky and Daniel protested. 'Rocks are boring.'

'Don't be silly,' lectured Merlin. 'You can learn a lot from a rock. For example, did you know there are three main types?'

'No,' admitted the children unenthusiastically.

'There's sedimentary rock,' Merlin began, pointing to a stripy bit of stone. 'It's made from layers of tiny bits of rock, or sand, or shell. The layers get squashed together as new material presses on top, and it turns to rock.'

'It's easy to spot, because of the layers,' said Daniel.

'Exactly. Next, igneous rocks. They start out as hot, liquid rock from beneath the Earth's surface,' Merlin went on. 'When a volcano erupts, this liquid stuff comes to the surface. It cools off and forms really hard rock.' He tapped a bit of sparkly grey stone. 'This is granite – and it's a common igneous rock.'

'You can tell because it's hard,' murmured Becky.

'You've got it,' nodded Merlin. 'The third main type of rock is metamorphic. Metamorphic rocks start out as igneous or sedimentary rocks, but they get changed by being squeezed or heated up inside the Earth.' He tapped a hard, shiny white rock shot through with pink veins. 'This is marble – and it's a classic metamorphic rock.'

Daniel and Becky were surprised. 'It's quite interesting, really.'

'I told you so,' laughed Merlin. 'And by the way, when you're looking at rocks, keep an eye out for fossils. Fossils are the shapes of animals or plants that died millions of years ago. They got covered in layers of sand, and eventually their bony parts turned into rock and their soft parts rotted away to leave an impression of their shape. In fact, I think we'll have a fossil puzzle before we learn about climate.'

Fossil Puzzle
Fossil hunter Rock Hard has just uncovered this amazing fossil of a dinosaur's bones. Which dinosaur was it?

PTERODACTYL

BRONTOSAURUS

DIPLODOCUS

If you choose . . .	Turn to the world map and cross out . . .
Pterodactyl	3
Brontosaurus	38
Diplodocus	18

Hot Spots

'Put on your sunglasses and hats,' warned Merlin as they arrived at their next destination.

'We're in the middle of a desert,' observed Daniel.

'And it's hot!' exclaimed Becky.

'That's because this is the Sahara Desert, and it's not far from the Equator. The Equator is an imaginary line round the middle of the Earth.'

'Why is it so hot?' Becky asked. She touched the sand. It was burning.

'Because the Equator faces the sun directly all year round and receives the full force of its rays. Places near the North and South Poles spend half the year turned away from the Sun,' Merlin explained. 'A diagram might help.' He drew one in the sand, using the tip of his wand. 'See how it works?' he asked.

Becky and Daniel nodded. 'The North and South Poles are furthest away from the Sun. That must be why they're so cold,' Daniel said.

'You've got it,' nodded Merlin. 'Some deserts, like this one, are very hot. Hot deserts are the driest places in the world. Some of them are sandy, like this one. Others are stony. Sometimes the rocks get carved into strange shapes by the wind.'

'Who lives in the desert?' Daniel asked.

'It's difficult for *anything* to live in the desert,' Merlin said. 'Without water nothing can grow. There *is* water, but it's a long way underground.' He pointed to a clump of trees in the distance. 'Sometimes the water appears on the surface and creates a pool. Trees grow round it and people can live there. It's called an oasis. Let's go and have a look at that one over there. And we'll have a puzzle before we move on to the rainforest.'

Hot Spot Puzzle
Here's a picture of the oasis visited by Merlin, Becky and Daniel. 'I think this place is deserted,' said Becky. But Merlin wasn't convinced.

'I think there are several people here,' he said. 'You can see them too if you look closely.'

How many people – not counting Merlin and the children – are there at the oasis?

If you choose ...	Turn to the world map and cross out ...
2 people	9
4 people	17
6 people	20

Rainforests

'It's a good job I remembered to bring my umbrella,' said Merlin when he and the children arrived at their next destination. They all sheltered beneath it as rain fell around them.

'Where are we?' asked Becky, peering out. They were in a dark, gloomy place. Tall trees stretched up far above them. Thick creepers and plants grew round their feet and there was a strong smell of wet earth and rotting vegetation.

'This is a tropical rainforest,' Merlin said. He wiped the sweat from his forehead.

'It's hot, isn't it?' said Daniel. 'And steamy!'

'That's right,' Merlin agreed. 'It's very close to the Equator, which is why it's so warm. All round the world, the areas closest to the Equator are covered in tropical rainforest.'

'The trees are *huge*,' exclaimed Becky.

'They grow thickly in this hot, steamy atmosphere,' explained Merlin. 'Every day there are storms like this one, so there's plenty of water.' Just then the rain stopped and he was able to put down the umbrella.

Above their heads something moved through the trees and a loud screaming noise made them jump. 'It's a monkey!' shouted Daniel.

'And there's a parrot!' Becky pointed upwards. Then a huge butterfly fluttered past – the biggest they'd ever seen.

'As you can see, the rainforest is a very interesting place. There are all sorts of things living here – including people,' Merlin told them. 'There are wonderful flowers and fruit, too. And other things that aren't so nice!' He pointed at a big snake coiled around a tree trunk.

'Maybe we'd better get out of here,' said Daniel nervously.

'OK,' nodded Merlin. 'But let's complete a puzzle before we go and explore a totally different climate!'

Rainforest Puzzle

In the word-search square below are hidden the names of several creatures or plants that live in the rainforests and other hot places. There's also the name of one creature that prefers snow and ice. How many heat-loving things can you find? The names all run in straight lines, across, up and down or diagonally. Some of them read back to front.

```
N H T O L S F N
A I F R P R A O
T S U I O H M I
O K D G N O L P
R E D A N E M R
R N R K M E B O
A I E A F T P C
P Y C A C T U S
```

If you choose . . .	Turn to the world map and cross out . . .
7 things	16
9 things	40
11 things	39

Cold Spots

'Brrr!' Becky and Daniel both shivered, even though they were now dressed in heavy coats with thick hats and boots – and so was Merlin.

'I thought we should take precautions against frostbite,' said Merlin with a smile. 'After all, we're now in Antarctica, near the South Pole, and it's one of the coldest regions on Earth.'

'What about the Arctic?' asked Becky. 'I get them muddled up.'

'The Arctic is a huge area of ice floating on the sea at the North Pole,' Merlin explained. 'Antarctica is a bit different. It's a vast piece of land covered in thick layers of ice and snow. Under the ice, coal and other minerals have been found. That indicates that once upon a time, trees and plants must have grown here.'

'In this cold weather?' Daniel looked around. There was nothing but snow to be seen.

'Millions of years ago the Earth's climate was different,' Merlin explained.

'At least it's sunny,' said Becky. She was right. The bright sunlight made the white ice and snow almost painfully bright.

'It's sunny because it's summer here,' Merlin went on. 'The South Pole is tipped towards the sun, and it doesn't get dark at all for six months of the year.'

'Six months!' Daniel exclaimed. Then he looked thoughtful. 'But when it does get dark, does it *stay* dark for six months?'

'That's right,' nodded Merlin. 'Winters here are pretty grim. Let's have another puzzle to keep us warm!'

Iceberg Puzzle

Here are some icebergs and information about where they come from. Which of these icebergs is from Antarctica?

Clues

Polar bears are found in the Arctic. Penguins aren't!
Icebergs from the South Pole usually have a flat top. Icebergs from the North Pole have pointed tops, like mountains.

If you choose . . .   Turn to the world map and cross out . . .

1	17
2	12
3	4
4	29
5	33

Coal and Oil

Becky was looking bothered. They were standing in front of some big buildings where a sign hung which read THE BURNSBETTA COAL COMPANY.

'Merlin, you said we could tell there had once been trees growing on Antarctica because scientists had found coal there,' said Becky. 'That doesn't make sense.'

'It does if you know something about coal,' smiled Merlin. 'Put these overalls on, both of you, and we'll go down the mine and take a closer look.'

The children climbed into their overalls and put crash helmets on their heads. Then they got into a lift that whisked them down to the bottom of the shaft. Merlin led them to a thick seam of glittery black coal.

'Millions of years ago,' he began, 'the Earth's surface was covered in forests and swamps.' The children nodded. 'Over thousands of years, the trees fell down into the swamps. New ones grew – and they fell on top of the first ones, and it went on like that for ages.'

Daniel nodded. 'But where does coal come into it?' he asked.

'I'm just getting to that. The swamp water was acidic,' Merlin explained. 'It preserved the wood. Gradually, after millions more years, the climate changed. Layers of sand and rock built up over the layers of dead trees. The trees got slowly squeezed – and turned into coal.'

'Oh!' Becky and Daniel were surprised. They touched the hard, black coal. It was strange to think it had once been wood.

'Oil is formed in the same kind of way,' Merlin

continued. 'Millions of years ago the sea was full of tiny creatures so small you could hardly see them. When they died, they fell to the bottom of the ocean and got buried in the mud. The mud hardened, and the bodies of the dead creatures turned into tiny drops of oil. Today, we drill down into the ground and the oil comes gushing up.'

'And we use it to make petrol!' finished Daniel.

'And for plastics and all sorts of other things,' nodded Merlin. 'I think perhaps our next destination should be the ocean. But before we go, you've got another puzzle to tackle!'

Coal-mining Puzzle
Here's a picture of a coal mine. Three miners, Ted, Fred and Ned, have finished their shift and want to get to the surface. They've each decided to take a different route. Whose journey is the shortest?

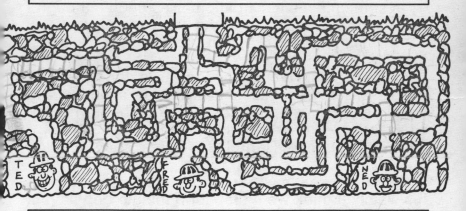

If you choose . . .	Turn to the world map and cross out . . .
Ted's	10
Fred's	1
Ned's	21

Oceans

'This is amazing!' giggled Becky. She, Merlin and Daniel were bobbing around in the ocean, safe inside a big bubble. 'How did you do it?'

'Just a bit of magic,' said Merlin modestly. 'But enough of that – we're here to learn about the ocean!'

The bubble descended through the water. Gradually it became dark and the creatures swimming around them looked strange and unfamiliar. 'Seven tenths of the Earth's surface is covered by water,' Merlin began. 'The deeper we go, the more weight of water there is on top of us. This is called water pressure. Fish who live deep down, with a lot of pressure, are often flat – like that one there.' He pointed at a big flat fish.'

'How deep is the ocean?' Becky asked.

'In some places it's 11 kilometres deep – though I don't think we'll go right to the bottom today.'

'Oh,' sighed Daniel. Then he thought of a question. 'Why is the sea salty?'

'Because as rivers flow towards the sea, the water runs over rocks and dissolves chemicals in them. One of these chemicals is salt. That's why the sea is salty – and gradually getting saltier.'

'Yuck!' laughed Daniel. 'It tastes salty enough already!'

Merlin stroked his beard thoughtfully and checked his watch. 'I think we'll stop for a minute and have a quick puzzle. And when you've done that, we can go on and take a look at some of the amazing things that live under the sea.'

Ocean Puzzle

Christy Columbo, world-famous windsurfer, plans to surf her way round the world. She's going to start from Australia and surf west, around the southern coast of Africa. Then she's heading north up the coast of South America to the Panama Canal. She'll surf through the canal and out the other side, then head back towards Australia. Which oceans will she surf across, and in what order? You can use your own atlas to help work it out!

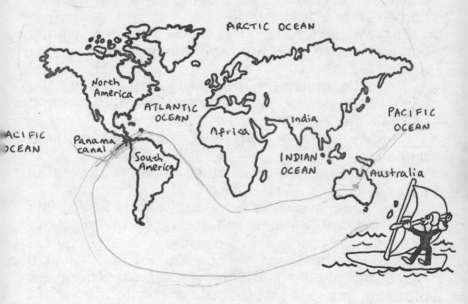

If you choose ...	Turn to the world map and cross out ...
Pacific, Atlantic, Indian	15
Indian, Arctic, Mediterranean, Atlantic	22
Indian, Atlantic, Pacific	5

Under the Sea

Becky and Daniel peered out of the bubble. Far beneath them, the bottom of the sea stretched out in huge cliffs and deep valleys, connected by wide plains of flat land. Whales and dolphins swam around, surrounded by shoals of fish.

'I thought the bottom of the sea was flat and smooth, like a beach!' Becky said, amazed.

Merlin laughed. 'Oh, no! The bottom of the sea is just like the land. It has mountains and volcanoes and all sorts of features.'

The two children stared, wide-eyed, as a huge octopus swam by. 'Are we safe in here?' Becky whispered.

'Perfectly,' nodded Merlin. 'The octopus can't see us. The octopus is just one of the useful plants and animals that live in the ocean.'

'There's cod, for fish and chips,' Daniel suggested.

'Yes, cod and dozens of other kinds of fish,' Merlin agreed.

'And squid and octopus to eat,' added Becky. 'My mum and dad have that when they go on holiday to Greece.'

Merlin nodded again. 'But it's not just fish and crabs and shellfish, which we can eat. There are other things. Sponges, for instance. Natural sponges grow in the ocean and are picked so we can use them in the bath. And then there's seaweed. That's harvested and turned into fertilizers for the land, and a kind of jelly used in ice-cream and other foods.'

Daniel pulled a face. 'They put seaweed in ice-cream?'

'Yes,' said Merlin. 'And of course, there's oil and natural gas under the sea too. But we have to be careful not to take too much from our oceans or pollute them with chemicals. In some parts of the world, fishermen have caught all the fish and there are none left. And dolphins and whales and other creatures are being killed. If we're not careful, all the life in our seas will die.'

'That would be terrible,' said Becky sadly.

Merlin cheered them up. 'Here's another puzzle for you to tackle,' he said. 'And when you've finished that, I think we'll go for a swim in some very strange seas!'

Underwater Puzzle
There are lots of creatures living in the sea, as you can see! How many matching pairs can you find in this picture?

If you choose . . .	Turn to the world map and cross out . . .
4	6
6	⑧
8	26

Strange Seas

'I can swim! I've learnt to swim!' spluttered Daniel, splashing around in the water.

'And I'm floating!' squealed Becky. 'I couldn't float before.'

Before Merlin could explain, Daniel swallowed a mouthful of water. 'Ugh!' he complained. 'This water is the saltiest I've ever tasted!'

'It's six times saltier than normal seawater, to be precise,' said Merlin, who was wearing a splendid black swimsuit decorated with stars. 'That's because we've come to the Dead Sea, between Israel and Jordan.'

'Why is it so salty?' Becky asked.

'Because several salty rivers flow into it, but none flows out,' Merlin explained. 'It's very hot here, so every day lots of water evaporates and leaves its salt behind. Each year the sea gets saltier and saltier.'

'Is that why it's so easy to swim?' Daniel asked, splashing about.

'That's right. The saltier water is, the easier it is for us to float. Here in the Dead Sea, it's quite difficult to drown,' laughed Merlin. 'There are other strange facts about seas too. Take the Mediterranean, for example,' he went on. 'About six million years ago it was a sea. Then it got blocked off at the narrow point where it meets the Atlantic Ocean. The water dried up and it turned into a desert. But then a million or so years later, the waves from the Atlantic broke through the blockage, and it filled up with water again!'

'I'm pleased about that,' grinned Daniel, 'because Mum and Dad are taking me to Spain for a holiday, and I want to try swimming in the Mediterranean.'

'Well, wear your armbands,' advised Merlin. 'You won't float as well there.' After they'd swum for a little while longer, he stood up. 'I think it's time for another puzzle – and then we'll take a look at coastlines.'

Strange Seas Puzzle
Only one river flows from the Itt Sea to the Bit Sea. Which one is it?

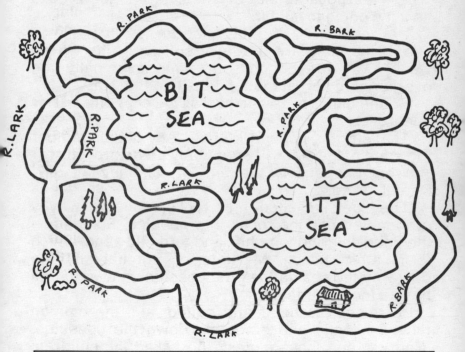

If you choose . . .	Turn to the world map and cross out . . .
River Bark	5
River Lark	32
River Park	34

Coastlines

'Wow! Look down there!' Becky and Daniel leaned out from the basket that hung beneath their hot-air balloon and looked at the sea and rocks below.

'Just as I thought,' said Merlin with a satisfied smile. 'This is going to be an excellent way of learning about the coast.'

'Look at those huge cliffs,' Daniel cried, pointing. 'There's a house built very near the edge. It looks as if it's going to fall off.'

'I expect it will, one day,' Merlin told them. 'You see, if the cliffs are made of soft rock, the waves wear away the bottom part, and eventually the overhanging part at the top falls into the sea.'

'So the cliff moves backwards?' Becky raised her eyebrows.

'That's right,' nodded Merlin. 'Any buildings near the edge of the cliff will eventually be destroyed.'

'What happens to the bits of cliff that fall off?' Daniel asked.

'They get smashed into rocks, and the waves gradually break the rocks into pebbles. Sometimes the pebbles grind together and turn into sand, which forms a nice beach,' Merlin said. 'But that's not the only way the sea shapes the coastline. Let's go and have a look over there.'

He raised his head and puffed, and the balloon moved silently and smoothly down the coastline. 'Can you see those caves?' he asked the children. They nodded.

'The waves rush into cracks in the rock and slowly make a bigger and bigger hole. If the headland is narrow, the cave may go all the way through the rock to form an arch – like that one there.' Merlin

36

pointed to an arch. Beyond it stood two tall stacks of rock.

'I bet that used to be an arch, till the middle part collapsed,' said Daniel.

'Ten out of ten!' laughed Merlin. 'Seeing as you know so much about coastlines, Daniel, why don't you try this puzzle?'

Coastline Puzzle
Christy Columbo is travelling along this stretch of coastline on her windsurfer. She goes round the stacks and past the spit and stops for a breather just past the first river estuary she comes to. What is the name of the place she stops at?

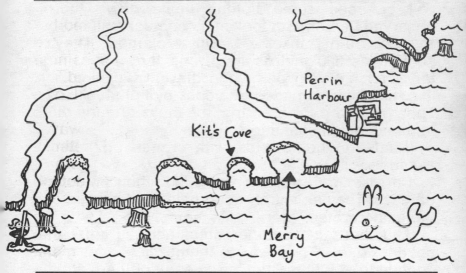

If you choose . . .	*Turn to the world map and cross out . . .*
Merry Bay	*11*
Perrin Harbour	*28*
Kit's Cove	*29*

Ports and Shipping

'Why have we come here?' asked Becky. The balloon had carried them along the coast until they arrived at a busy port.

'We're here to make you think!' exclaimed Merlin. 'Now, where would be the best place to build a port?'

'Somewhere the sea isn't rough,' Becky mused.

'That's right,' nodded Merlin. 'Many ports are built in sheltered bays or in the mouths of rivers, so that they're protected from rough weather. Some ports started as fishing villages and grew bigger over the years.'

'I can see some fishing boats down there,' observed Daniel. 'But look at those huge ships!'

'They are oil tankers,' Merlin explained. 'They're sometimes 300 metres long, and they have huge tanks for carrying oil. When they arrive at a port like this, they're guided into dock by little tug boats. Then pipes are lowered into the tanks and the oil is pumped out and put into storage.'

'What are those ships with cranes on?' Becky asked.

'Cargo ships. They carry goods in their holds and on deck. They have cranes to help load and unload the heavy crates,' Merlin told them.

'And that's a container ship there.' Daniel had spotted one. 'They carry things in huge metal containers. When they've been unloaded, the containers are put on wheels and attached to the backs of trucks.'

'That's right!' Merlin smiled. 'How do you know all this?'

'Simple,' grinned Daniel. 'My dad's a truck driver. He often drives container lorries!'

'In that case, you should have no trouble at all with this puzzle,' said Merlin.

Port Puzzle
It's a busy day at Grimsbottom, an east coast port. How many ships can you see being loaded or unloaded?

If you choose . . .	Turn to the world map and cross out . . .
5	16
6	28
8	31

Mountains

'Now I think we'll head inland and take a look at some mountains,' said Merlin. He puffed, and the balloon sailed through the air above the port and over the land, till some huge mountains loomed up in front of them.

'Remember what we learned about the plates that float over the Earth, like giant jigsaw pieces?' Merlin asked. The children nodded. 'Well, when two huge plates bump into each other, the land gets squeezed to make –'

'Mountains!' the children cried.

'That's right,' grinned Merlin. 'And remember, mountains exist under the sea as well as on land. In fact, what we call "land" is really just the tops of huge mountains that rise above the sea.'

The children looked impressed. 'I never thought of it like that,' murmured Becky.

'There's another kind of mountain over here,' Merlin announced. Once more the balloon set off. In the distance was a huge, cone-shaped mountain with a big crater in the top. Every so often, a puff of smoke rose from it.

'A volcano!' exclaimed Becky.

'Right again,' nodded Merlin. 'Volcanoes exist in places where the surface crust of the Earth is cracked. At a weak point, the red-hot liquid rock which forms the Earth's core can break through the surface. A volcano can start as a crack in the ground. Hot ash comes out of it to form a mound. Slowly, the mound grows into a mountain. Sometimes it explodes and throws gas and ash and liquid rock into the air.'

Daniel eyed the puffs of smoke rising from the

volcano's crater. 'Hadn't we better get out of here before it explodes?' he asked.

'Good idea,' agreed Merlin. 'And while we're getting back down to earth, you can have a go at this puzzle . . .'

Mountain Puzzle
Here's a picture of a mountain range. Imagine that after a terrible flood, the sea level rises to 1,500 metres. What would you see then?

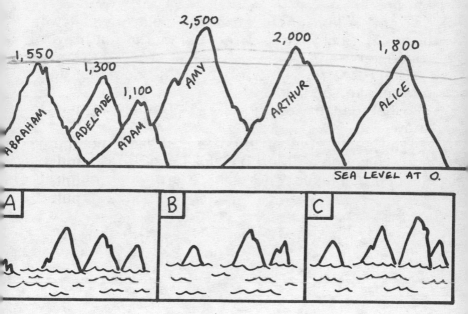

If you choose . . .	Turn to the world map and cross out . . .
A	22
B	14
C	23

Earthquakes

Merlin brought the balloon in for a gentle landing in a field. 'That was fun,' laughed Becky as they climbed out of the basket, 'but it's nice to be back on the ground again.'

Just at that moment, there was a low, rumbling sound, and the earth beneath their feet began to shake slightly. 'I wonder if that volcano's exploded?' Daniel asked.

'It feels more like an earthquake to me,' said Merlin.

'I saw a film about an earthquake once. It was horrible.' Becky was scared, but Merlin put his arm round her.

'Don't worry, it was only a demonstration earthquake,' he said.

'What causes earthquakes?' Daniel wanted to know.

'The same kind of thing that causes mountains and volcanoes,' Merlin told them. 'Earthquakes happen at places where there are weak points in

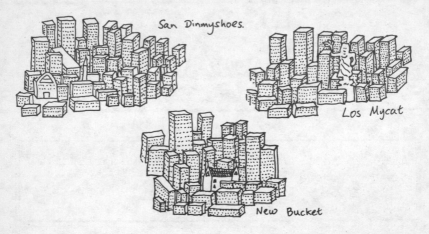

San Dinmyshoes.

Los Mycat

New Bucket

the Earth's crust, or where two plates meet.' He stamped his foot. The children copied him.

'The ground feels solid under our feet, doesn't it?' he said. Becky and Daniel nodded. 'That's because there's a thick layer of rock. But when those huge plates rub together, a patch of rock sometimes breaks. Then there's a big shock wave and everything on the surface gets jiggled around.'

'And that's what makes buildings fall over?' Becky asked.

'That's right,' nodded Merlin. 'And if the earthquake's at sea, or it's a big shock, the sea gets jiggled too. Sometimes that creates huge tidal waves, which flood low-lying areas and sink ships. All in all, it's best to avoid earthquakes if you can. But earthquake puzzles are perfectly safe!'

Earthquake Puzzle
A major earthquake has just hit a big city on the west coast of America. Here's a picture showing the damage. Which city was hit by the quake?

If you choose . . .	Turn to the world map and cross out . . .
San Dinmyshoes	13
Los Mycat	31
New Bucket	37

43

Rainy Weather

'It's raining!' Becky said as they set off across the field. 'I hate rain.'

Merlin looked surprised. 'But rain is so important! Without it, trees and plants would die – and so would people.'

'Where does rain come from?' Daniel asked as they sheltered under a tree.

'First let me ask *you* something,' Merlin said. 'When your mum hangs her washing out to dry, what do you think happens to the water in the clothes?'

Daniel shrugged. 'It just disappears,' he said.

'It has to go somewhere!' Merlin laughed. 'Actually, it evaporates. The heat of the sun turns the water into an invisible vapour, which rises up into the sky. It happens all the time. After it rains, the water evaporates from the pavements. It evaporates from seas and rivers too and goes up into the sky.'

'Then what happens?' Becky wanted to know.

'As it rises, the vapour gets colder and condenses into tiny droplets which hang in the air as clouds.'

'Like those up there,' giggled Daniel, pointing at the dark clouds.

'That's right,' nodded Merlin. 'Gradually lots of tiny droplets get stuck together to make one raindrop. Raindrops are heavy and fall to the Earth as rain. If it's really cold, the drops turn to hail or snowflakes.'

Becky looked out from under the tree. The rain had stopped and the sun was peeping through the clouds. 'So now it's finished raining,' she said, 'the raindrops on the grass will begin to evaporate and form new clouds –'

'And the cycle will begin again!' laughed Merlin.

'I can see you two have got the idea. Let's have a weather puzzle before we go on.'

'What's the next subject going to be?' Daniel asked.

Merlin smiled. 'I think it's about time we took a trip into space, and had a look at time.'

Cloud Puzzle
You can tell what the weather is going to be like by the clouds in the sky. Look at the four types of cloud described below. They all float at different levels in the sky, some low, some high. Following the clues, work out which type of cloud floats lowest.

Clues
Nimbostratus clouds float below flat cumulus clouds. Cirrus clouds float highest. Altocumulus clouds float above flat cumulus clouds.

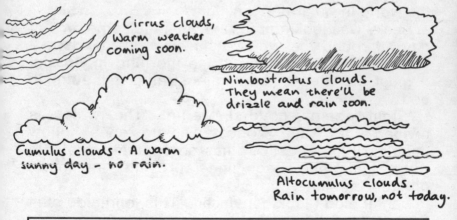

Cirrus clouds, warm weather coming soon.

Nimbostratus clouds. They mean there'll be drizzle and rain soon.

Cumulus clouds. A warm sunny day - no rain.

Altocumulus clouds. Rain tomorrow, not today.

If you choose . . .	Turn to the world map and cross out . . .
Altocumulus	24
Nimbostratus	37
Flat cumulus	32

Time

'Why do we need to travel into space to study time?' Becky asked, as the three travellers hovered above the Earth.

'Because time is related to the Earth's orbit,' Merlin explained. 'The Earth spins round once every twenty-four hours. You can't feel it when you're down there, but it's always moving. Now I'd like you to take a look at the Sun.'

He pointed in the direction of the Sun. 'Can you see how one side of the Earth is in sunlight, while the other half is dark?'

'Yes,' nodded Daniel. Then he had a brainwave. 'Does that mean that it's day on one side of the Earth, and night on the other?'

'That's right!' Merlin beamed. 'When Britain is experiencing day, for people on the other side of the world in Australia, it's night.'

Becky was looking puzzled. 'Is it the same time of day all round the world?' she wanted to know. 'I mean, if it's ten o'clock in the morning in Britain, it must be late at night in Australia, if they're in bed . . .'

'Right again,' nodded Merlin. 'The world is divided into time zones. These zones follow imaginary lines, called lines of longitude, that run round the globe. Each line represents an hour's difference in time.'

Daniel didn't look convinced. 'This longitude stuff sounds difficult.'

'Maybe we'll take a look at that next,' Merlin said. 'But it's not really so difficult. All you really need to know is that if you travel east from Britain, towards Japan, each time you cross a line of longitude you put your watch *forward* an hour. If you're going west, towards the USA, you put your watch *back* an hour each time you cross a line.'

Auntie Madge's Puzzle
Christy Columbo is in Britain. She wants to phone her Auntie Madge, who lives in Brisbane, Australia. It is 6 p.m. in Britain. Use the information below to decide what time it is in Brisbane.

If you choose . . .	Turn to the world map and cross out . . .
4 a.m.	30
11 p.m.	21
8 a.m.	36

Earth Lines

The next thing the children knew, they were back in their geography classroom at school. There was no one else around. 'What are we doing here?' asked Becky and Daniel in surprise.

'Everything we need to help us understand latitude and longitude is here,' Merlin told them. He opened a cupboard door. 'Ah, here's a map and a globe.' He put them on a table and opened out the map.

'Are these the lines of longitude?' Becky pointed at some fine lines drawn down the map, from the North Pole to the South Pole.

'That's right,' Merlin nodded. 'And these lines that run around the world are called lines of latitude. The one that goes round the middle of the Earth is called the Equator. The countries nearest the Equator are some of the hottest in the world. The further away you travel from the Equator, the cooler it's likely to be.'

'What are these numbers on the lines?' Daniel had been looking closely. 'This one says 15°.'

'Each line of latitude and longitude has a different number,' Merlin explained. 'The line of the Equator is described as 0° Latitude. There are other lines running above it and below it at 15° intervals. They have a number, followed by the description north or south, so you can tell if they are above or below the Equator.'

'The lines of longitude have numbers, too,' Becky spotted.

'Yes,' Merlin nodded. 'They are divided up into 15° intervals too, followed by the description east or west, so you can tell if they are to the left or right of the 0° line. Using the lines of latitude and longitude, you can pinpoint any place in the world.'

'I think I understand,' Daniel said, looking at the globe.

'Well, let's try a puzzle and see,' Merlin suggested.

Earth Lines Puzzle
Look at these three globes. One shows you the lines of latitude, another the lines of longitude, and on the third one, you'll see windsurfing champ Christy Columbo at a point where a line of latitude and a line of longitude meet. Which point is this?

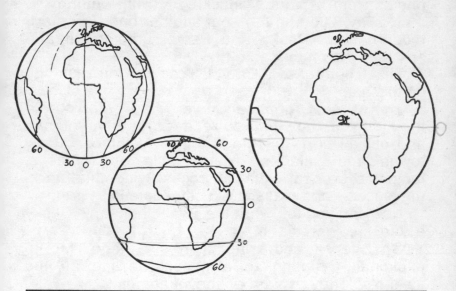

If you choose . . .	Turn to the world map and cross out . . .
60° north, 60° east	40
0°, 0°	12
30° south, 30° west	8

Maps for Beginners

'Have a look at this,' said Merlin, pulling a ragged bit of old parchment out of his pocket.

'What is it?' Becky and Daniel wondered. It showed a blotchy outline of an island, with strange monsters in the sea.

'It's an ancient map,' Merlin said, 'It's actually a map of Britain.'

'But it doesn't look anything *like* Britain!' Daniel laughed.

'Well, it's difficult to make an accurate map if you have no scientific instruments and you can't take photos from a plane,' chuckled Merlin, putting the map away. Then he took out another one – a smart, modern map. Becky and Daniel unfolded it and spread it out on the table.

'That's better,' said Daniel. 'I can see lots of things on this map.'

'This is an Ordnance Survey map,' Merlin told them. 'If you know how to read it properly, you can find out all sorts of things. Maps like these show towns and villages, roads, hills and valleys, footpaths, woods, cliffs, churches, windmills, parking places – and masses of useful details.'

'How can you tell what the symbols mean?' Becky asked, studying them.

'On every good map there's a key,' Merlin explained, pointing to a panel showing all the symbols. 'They explain all the meanings.'

'What are all these little brown lines?' Daniel pointed to them. 'Some are close together and some are further apart.'

'Ah, they're contour lines,' Merlin explained. 'They link up all the places that are the same height above sea level. Somewhere along the contour lines, you'll see a number which indicates how high they are. From the contour lines, you can work out where there are hills and valleys.'

'I think this is a hill,' Becky said, pointing to some lines.

'Why not have a go at this map puzzle?' Merlin suggested. 'And then we'll learn some more about map-reading.'

Map-making Puzzle
Here's a snapshot of the village of Poltacks. Which of the three maps is the most accurate representation of the area? They may not all be the right way up!

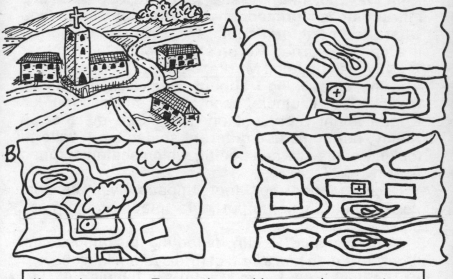

If you choose . . .	Turn to the world map and cross out . . .
Map A	14
Map B	29
Map C	24

Map-reading

'Now,' said Merlin, 'imagine I gave you a huge map of somewhere you didn't know, with every town and city and major road marked on it. And then I asked you to find a specific place. What would you do?'

'I'd look all over the map,' Becky answered with a shrug.

'It might take a long time,' Daniel added.

'But if I gave you just a bit more information, you'd be able to find it quickly,' Merlin revealed with a smile. He unfolded another map. It was crammed with towns and roads and information.

Becky frowned. 'It would help if you held it the right way up, Merlin,' she told him. 'Look at this little compass printed on the map. It shows you where the north and south are. North should be at the top.' She turned Merlin's map round for him.

'Silly me,' beamed Merlin. 'I should have checked. And the other thing I should check is the scale of the map. For example, each centimetre distance on a map might represent one kilometre distance in reality, but maps use different scales, so it's worth looking at the key and seeing which scale your map is drawn to.'

Becky tapped her foot impatiently. 'But that doesn't help us find a particular place on the map,' she complained.

'I forgot,' said Merlin, twiddling his moustache. 'Look, this map has a kind of grid system laid out over it. The lines from top to bottom are labelled A, B, C and so on. Those reading across the map are labelled 1, 2, 3, and so on. Now, if I told you that the place I want you to find is situated at the place where line A crosses line 3, it wouldn't take you long to find it.'

'Give us a puzzle and we'll see if the grid system works,' challenged Becky.

'Here it is,' smiled Merlin. 'And when you've finished, I think we'll go exploring!'

Map-reading Puzzle
Here's a map. Your challenge is to find a village called Kell, 20 kilometres north of Horerr. The map reference for Horerr is C3. Which of the three villages is Kell?

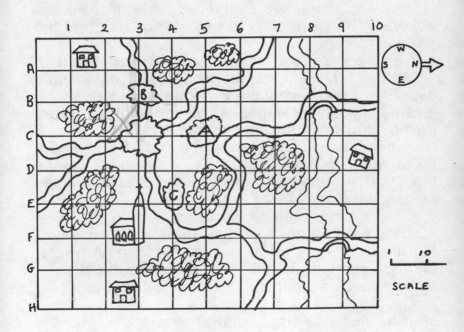

If you choose . . .   Turn to the world map and cross out . . .

A	9
B	26
C	32

Early Explorers

'I didn't think you meant *this* kind of exploring!' laughed Daniel. He, Becky and Merlin were standing at the prow of a huge old sailing ship. Her timbers creaked and sails cracked as they plunged through the waves.

'Who's the captain?' Becky asked, looking up to the deck where an imposing figure was staring out to sea.

'That's Christopher Columbus,' Merlin told the children. 'He's probably the most famous of all the early explorers.'

'He discovered America,' Daniel said confidently.

'Well . . .' Merlin looked troubled. 'That's what everyone says, but people were already living there, and by the time Columbus arrived in 1492, other Europeans had already made the journey. A Norwegian called Leif Ericsson started a settlement there about 500 years earlier. And some people think that an Irish monk called Saint Brendan sailed across 400 years before Columbus.'

'Oh.' Daniel looked disappointed.

'They didn't have accurate maps in those days,' Merlin went on, 'so when he reached the West Indies, Columbus thought he'd reached China!'

'He sounds a bit muddled,' said Becky.

'Oh, no – he was a brave explorer,' protested Merlin. 'In those days, many people believed the world was flat like a plate. They warned him he'd fall off the edge if he sailed too far, but he didn't believe them.'

'What about Sir Francis Drake?' Daniel asked. 'We did him in history.'

Merlin twirled his moustache. 'Drake sailed right

round the world, you know. It took him three years, with plenty of stops on the way. In fact,' he held up his finger, 'why don't we have a puzzle about Drake?'

Swashbuckling Puzzle

Here's Sir Francis Drake showing Queen Elizabeth all the amazing treasures he's brought back from his round-the-world trip. But hold on a minute — there are a few things that look a bit out of place! How many out-of-place items can you see in the picture?

If you choose . . .	Turn to the world map and cross out . . .
3	4
5	25
7	30

The Human Race

'I think', said Merlin, 'it's time we learned a bit more about our ancestors and where they came from. So . . .' He swirled his cloak and there was a bang and a flash, and the three time travellers found themselves in a cave. But this one wasn't like the cave Becky and Daniel had hidden in on their geography trip. This one had paintings on the walls.

'Is this where early people lived?' Daniel asked.

'Some of them,' said Merlin, sitting down on a rock. 'According to the scientists, all human beings developed from one group of people who lived in Africa.'

'How do they know?' Becky wondered.

'Because although human beings from different parts of the world look different, they have many more similarities than differences,' Merlin told them. 'This tribe of early people grew in numbers, and over thousands of years groups moved away from the area.'

Daniel looked puzzled. 'How did they cross the oceans?'

'In those days, some parts of the world that are now separated by oceans were joined together, so you could just walk from one continent to another. For example, one group of people travelled to Mongolia. From there, some set out and reached Canada and North America. Other groups moved north from Africa into Europe. It took millions of years.'

'But people have different colour skin,' Becky said.

'That happened slowly too,' Merlin explained. 'The people who live in very hot parts of the world, like Africa and Australia, developed dark skins as a protection against the sun. Those who lived in cold places, like Canada, developed narrow eyes to protect them from the cold.'

Becky grinned. 'So under our skins, we're all the same.'

'Precisely,' nodded Merlin. 'Time for another puzzle, I think – and then we're off to visit some rather special people.'

Human Race Puzzle

Early humans used to paint wonderful pictures on their cave walls. Many featured animals, on whom they depended for food. Here's an example of a cave painting. How many animals and people are going from the left to the right?

If you choose . . .	Turn to the world map and cross out . . .
9	15
13	6
16	28

Tribal Peoples

There was another flash and a bang, and Becky and Daniel found themselves in a clearing in the forest. Huge trees rose overhead. In front of them, in a clearing in the jungle, was a large hut made of wood, with a thatched roof. People were working around the hut. Women were preparing food, while the men made spears and arrows.

'Have we gone back in time to the past? Are these some of the early people you were talking about?' Becky asked.

'No,' said Merlin, shaking his head. 'We're right up to date. These are just a few of the tribal people who live around the world today, following the lifestyle and traditions that they've developed over hundreds and thousands of years.'

'You mean they don't have TV or cars?' Daniel was amazed when Merlin shook his head. 'What do they do?'

'They hunt and gather fruit and honey and fish and roots to eat. In some parts of the world, tribal people keep herds of cattle or goats,' Merlin explained. 'This is the kind of life that many of our ancestors led. We can learn a lot from the way they live in harmony with nature.'

'It's amazing!' Daniel breathed, watching some boys shooting arrows. 'But what'll happen to them?'

'With a bit of luck, they'll be left alone,' Merlin said sternly. 'In some places, so-called "civilized" people think that because these tribes don't have money, and don't speak their language, it's all right to take their land and ruin their way of life. But fortunately, other people realize that they have the right to continue their lives in the traditional way.

They've turned parts of this rainforest into reservations, so that the people who live here aren't disturbed.'

'That sounds like a good idea,' Becky and Daniel said.

'I agree,' nodded Merlin. 'So let's have a puzzle to celebrate – and then let's explore a different type of life.'

House-building Puzzle
Divad is getting married next month to his girlfriend Gimya, and he and his friends have just finished building their new house. It took Divad and all his friends, together with their fathers, a week to build the house. According to custom, Divad bows four times to his friends and six times to the four fathers to thank them for their help. He bows 56 times in all. How many friends helped Divad?

If you choose . . .	Turn to the world map and cross out . . .
8 friends	15
4 friends	31
6 friends	9

Towns and Cities

'It's really noisy here after the rainforest!' shouted Becky, putting her fingers in her ears. They'd just arrived on a busy city street. Above them rose tall buildings, and traffic thundered all around them.

'If tribal life is one extreme way of living, this is another,' said Merlin crossly, narrowly avoiding being run over by a bicycle. 'Millions of people around the world live in cities.'

'How did we get from tribal life to this?' shouted Daniel.

'Well,' said Merlin, leading the children to a safer and quieter spot in a park, 'it took a very long time.'

'Like everything!' laughed Becky.

'You're learning,' nodded Merlin. 'To start with, people lived in small villages, growing their own food and making the things they needed. Then, gradually, they began to make things to sell to one another. They'd meet at one village to exchange these things. Perhaps one person would swap two chickens for a pair of shoes.'

'That sounds like a bargain,' giggled Becky.

'You could get a lot for a couple of chickens in those days,' Merlin said wisely. 'Anyway, soon there would be a regular market. And once there was a market, visitors came and people opened up businesses there. Those who liked a bit of bustle would leave the countryside and live in town. A big church might be built there, and then perhaps a school.'

'And roads,' Daniel reminded him, as a taxi beeped its horn loudly.

'And roads,' Merlin echoed, 'and later perhaps a railway. And before you knew what had happened, in a thousand years or so a tiny village was transformed into a place like this!' He waved his hand round at the buildings. 'Time for a town puzzle – and then we'll visit a city from the past!'

Town Puzzle
Here's a picture of Puddleton-on-the-Marsh, Christy Columbo's home town. Can you find Park View, the house that Christy's great-grandfather built? It's the second house along from the church. You get there over the bridge from the High Street. We've given you three suggestions – A, B or C!

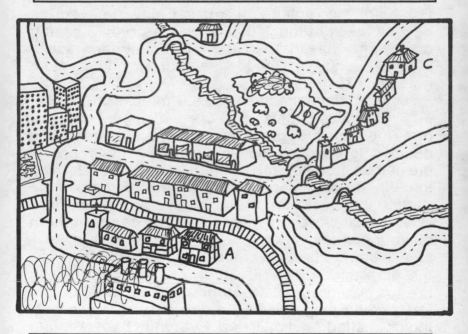

If you choose . . .	Turn to the world map and cross out . . .
A	19
B	1
C	22

Vanished Civilizations

'At least it's quieter here,' murmured Daniel, looking round at a series of huge ruined buildings set among trees in the jungle. In some places the buildings were almost completely covered with creepers and undergrowth. In others, they could see the remains of impressive statues and temples.

'It's spooky,' shivered Becky, despite the fact that it was hot and steamy. 'Where are we?'

'We're in Mexico,' Merlin told the children, 'and these are the remains of a great Mayan city. In its heyday, back in the 1400s, it was a pretty amazing place. The Mayans had their own religions and a calendar, and they made beautiful art objects from gold and precious stones.'

'So what happened to them?' Daniel asked.

'In the 1500s Spanish explorers arrived. They took one look at the gold and precious jewels and decided to conquer the whole area. Thousands of the native people were killed and others just ran into the forest to hide. Over hundreds of years some of the cities were forgotten, but most of them were later rediscovered. In your time, you can visit them on your holidays.'

'Are there other lost cities?' Becky asked.

'Lots,' nodded Merlin. 'For example, in 1861 a French explorer called Henri Mouhot was in the Cambodian jungle when he came across an amazing city called Angkor Thom. Everyone had forgotten about it for four hundred years.'

Daniel's eyes lit up. 'I'd like to be an explorer and find some lost cities.'

'OK,' said Merlin. 'Why not start now with a puzzle?'

Lost Cities Puzzle

The Incas, Aztecs and Mayans of Mexico and South America built pyramid-shaped temples. Here are two flat plans of one of their pyramids. Which of the three below fits both plans?

If you choose . . .   Turn to the world map and cross out . . .
          A   27
          B   6
          C   15

Countries

Merlin sat down on the steps of a Mayan temple, pulled a map out from his robe and unfolded it.

'It's a map of the world,' Daniel said.

'You're a genius, Daniel!' Merlin joked. 'As you're so clever, tell me what the different coloured bits are.'

'They're countries of course,' Daniel replied. 'This is easy!'

'And how did they get to be countries?' Merlin asked.

'Hmmm,' said Daniel. 'That's more difficult.'

'Then let me explain,' Merlin smiled. 'There are more than 150 countries in the world, but the number can change. Sometimes, as a result of a war or a political agreement, one country is absorbed into another. Later, those countries may separate into individual states again. You've probably seen this happening recently, when the country we used to call the USSR divided into the smaller states it was made up of.'

'I saw the news about it on TV,' Becky chipped in. 'My mum says we have to learn the new names for the countries.'

'She's right,' nodded Merlin. 'Countries sometimes change their name. The country we call Sri Lanka was once called Ceylon. But names are only one thing that distinguishes countries from each other.'

'Yeah,' said Daniel. 'Different countries have different money.'

'That's right,' Merlin agreed. 'And usually each country has its own government and makes its own rules. They have their own stamps too.'

'And passports,' added Becky.

'And flags!' Daniel remembered.

'That sounds like an ideal subject for another puzzle,' said Merlin. 'And then let's go and see some of the world's great sights.'

Flag Puzzle

Here are pictures of five flags. Four of them are national flags, one is not. Use the clues to decide which is the odd one out.

Clues

Australia has two more stars than New Zealand. Turkey's got just one star. The USA's got more stars than anyone else.

If you choose . . .	Turn to the world map and cross out . . .
Flag 1	2
Flag 2	7
Flag 3	23
Flag 4	33
Flag 5	40

Sightseeing Tour

'Hey, we're in a helicopter!' Daniel exclaimed, as Merlin swept the children off for their next adventure.

'It's a great way of sightseeing,' Merlin said as he brought the helicopter down a little. 'Look over there. What do you see?'

'The Pyramids!' Becky shouted. 'This must be Egypt.'

'Got it in one,' Merlin beamed. 'There are some places so famous that everyone recognizes them. And they all recognize the Great Pyramid of Cheops. It was built 5,000 years ago. It's made of $2\frac{1}{2}$ million stone blocks and they were all dragged here, because at that time no one had thought of inventing the wheel!' The children laughed. 'Now let's fast-forward to another famous place,' Merlin said. He pressed the turbo-drive button and the world whizzed past beneath them.

'This is no ordinary helicopter,' Daniel gasped.

'When was I ever ordinary?' Merlin joked. 'Ah, we're here.' He pressed another switch and the helicopter slowed down.

'It's Stonehenge,' Becky announced, looking down.

'Right again,' laughed Merlin. 'Another world-famous monument. It's not as old as the Pyramids. It was only built about 3,000 years ago.'

'But what was it built for?' Daniel asked.

'I'm not allowed to say,' Merlin told them. 'We time lords have to keep some things shrouded in mystery. But scientists think it may have been a kind of computer for recording sunrise and sunset and calculating the date.' He looked at his watch.

'Oh dear,' he sighed. 'I'd hoped to fit in a trip to the Great Wall of China and the leaning tower of Pisa, too, but we've run out of time. We'll just have to do another puzzle instead.'

Sightseeing Puzzle
Here are Christy Columbo's snapshots of some of the famous places she's visited. She's also made a list of the countries they are in – but unfortunately there's a mistake in the list. One of the countries is wrong. Which one? You can use an encyclopaedia or a textbook to find out.

ITALY
FRANCE
AUSTRALIA

The Sydney Opera House

INDIA

St Paul's Cathedral   The Eiffel Tower

EGYPT

The Sphinx   The Taj Mahal

If you choose . . .	Turn to the world map and cross out . . .
India	8
Italy	34
France	16
Australia	24
Egypt	5

Language

'Slobi noz tooto Panki?' said Merlin as he landed the helicopter.

Becky and Daniel looked at each other. What was going on? 'We don't understand,' replied Becky.

'That's because I was speaking Panki – a language only spoken by the lost Hanki tribe,' Merlin said proudly. The children were suspicious.

'Why talk Panki?' they asked.

'Because languages are very important,' Merlin said. 'Did you know that more than 3,000 different languages are spoken all over the world? If we include all the local dialects, then it comes to about 10,000. In India the official language is Hindi, but only half the people use it.'

'So how do they speak to each other?' Becky asked.

'With difficulty,' chuckled Merlin. 'The origin of different languages is very interesting. English, which you speak, has lots of similarities with German and Dutch. There are also some links with French and Italian, which are based on an old language called Latin.'

'That was the Romans' language!' grinned Becky.

'That's right,' nodded Merlin. 'Anyway, experts say that both English and French belong to the Indo-European language family. They believe that these languages were brought by people from India, thousands of years ago. Gradually, as the people who spoke them divided into different groups and settled in different parts of Europe, they developed variations. But basically, all the languages in one language family follow the same kind of rules.'

Daniel had been thinking. 'What we need is a

new language everyone in the world could speak. Then we could all understand each other,' he said.

'That's a great idea – and it's already been tried,' Merlin told him. 'The famous "new" language is Esperanto, which was invented in the 1880s. It's thought that about 500,000 people can speak it. But this puzzle isn't about Esperanto!'

Language Puzzle

When explorers first arrived in Australia they were amazed at some of the creatures they saw. 'We've never seen one of those before. What do you call that?' they asked one of the native Australians, pointing to a particular creature.

'I don't know,' he said in his own language.

'Ah!' said the explorers, who didn't understand a word of it. 'So that's an "I don't know". Fascinating.'

They were looking at one of the animals pictured here. Can you work out what the Australian aboriginal word for 'I don't know' is?

If you choose . . .	Turn to the world map and cross out . . .
Kiwi	19
Sheep	27
Kangaroo	7

Writing

'It's not just language that makes for communication problems,' Becky said as they climbed down from the helicopter. 'Writing does, too. Just look at that sign over there. I can't read what it says.'

'That's because it's in Arabic,' Merlin explained. 'You're absolutely right, Becky. Different civilizations have invented different kinds of alphabet.'

'When did people first start writing?' Daniel wanted to know.

'About 5,000 years ago, according to the experts,' Merlin told him. 'In those days they didn't use paper and ink. They wrote on damp clay, using a stick. As writing developed, people invented their own symbols to represent sounds. The alphabet used for English and most other European languages is called the Roman alphabet.'

'I know there are twenty-six letters in our alphabet,' Daniel said, 'but do all the other languages have the same number?'

'No!' smiled Merlin. 'Take Chinese, for example. Chinese "letters" developed from pictures. If a person wanted to write about a bird, they drew a picture of a bird. Over many centuries, these pictures were turned into symbols. Instead of learning twenty-six letters which could be used to make any word, Chinese people had to learn 40,000 separate symbols to represent all the things around them.'

'*Forty thousand?*' The children could hardly believe it.

'That's right,' Merlin nodded. 'Fortunately, a few years ago it was decided that this was bit much. So the Chinese reorganized the language, and now most people learn a basic set of about 1,000 symbols.'

'I'm glad I don't have to learn them,' muttered Becky.

'I'm sure you're good at languages,' Merlin smiled. 'Why not try this puzzle and see?'

Writing Puzzle
Writing is a kind of code. Can you crack this code and find out where the treasure's hidden?

If you choose ...	Turn to the world map and cross out ...
Behind the mask	2
In the casket	23
Beneath the rocks	12

Money

The three time travellers walked away from the helicopter and down a dusty street.

'Where are we now?' Daniel asked. It was hot, and the people they saw were all wearing loose trousers or lengths of cotton fabric tied in sarongs.

'Somewhere in Thailand, I think,' said Merlin vaguely. A bit further along the road they came to a street market.

'Look over here!' called Becky. She was standing by a stall selling beautiful necklaces and jewellery. 'I'd like to buy one of these as a souvenir,' she decided, feeling in her pocket for her purse. But when she held out some coins, the woman behind the counter refused to take them.

'You've got to have the right currency,' Merlin explained. 'When you go abroad, you have to change the money you use in your own country – in your case, pounds – into the currency they use in the country you're visiting.'

'It would be easier if everyone used the same money,' Becky grumbled.

'That's true,' nodded Merlin. 'But money is a fairly recent invention. For a long time, people managed without it. They just swapped things with each other.'

'Why did they introduce money?' Daniel asked.

'Because sometimes bartering was difficult. If you wanted to swap two chickens for a pair of shoes, but the shoemaker didn't want your chickens, you were stuck. So people began to use coins to represent the value of their goods.'

'And does everyone use coins?' Becky wanted to know.

'Oh no.' Merlin shook his head. 'In some countries they used shells. In parts of Ethiopia, bars of salt are used instead of cash. Tell you what, let's have a money puzzle and see how much you know about different currencies.'

Money Puzzle
Listed below are some facts about currencies. From the details given, which of these wallets would give you the most spending power? (The figures are not necessarily accurate representations of actual currency values.)

Clues
You can get $2 for every £1.
There are about 120 yen to $1.
There are about 10 French francs in £1.
There are about 3 German Deutschmarks to 120 yen.

If you choose . . .	Turn to the world map and cross out . . .
Wallet A	5
Wallet B	10
Wallet C	38
Wallet D	14
Wallet E	35

Religions – Part 1

'What's that?' Daniel pointed to a beautiful golden statue standing on a rock near the market.

'That's the Buddha,' Merlin said. 'The people in Thailand follow the Buddhist religion.'

'Do all countries have their own religions?' Becky asked.

Merlin shook his head. 'No. There are a few main religions around the world, and thousands of variations. Buddhism, for example, started in India around 2,500 years ago. Buddhists believe that pain and suffering are caused by people's greed and selfishness. They try to lead a good life that doesn't harm anyone. They believe that they are born over and over again until they reach a stage of everlasting peace.'

'What about Christianity?' Becky asked.

'Well,' said Merlin, 'Christians believe that about 2,000 years ago God sent his son, Jesus Christ, to teach mankind how to lead good, peaceful lives. You can read about Jesus in the Bible. You'll find Christians wherever you go around the world. Christianity is the main religion of western Europe, North and South America and parts of Africa.'

'And Hinduism?' Daniel wanted to know. 'We learned something about it at school.'

'Hinduism is very interesting,' Merlin said. 'It's the oldest world religion. There are a lot of Hindu gods, and it's quite a complicated religion to understand. Most Hindus live in India. They believe in reincarnation, like the Buddhists, and hope one day they will be united with God. Hindus believe that cows are sacred creatures.'

'There's a lot to remember,' sighed Becky.

'And that's not half of it!' laughed Merlin. 'But before I tell you about some other religions, have a go at this puzzle.'

Religions Puzzle
How much do you know about the different religions of the world? Here are four religious symbols. Which one might you find in a Buddhist temple?

If you choose . . .	Turn to the world map and cross out . . .
A	16
B	39
C	21
D	7

Religions – Part 2

'Were you joking when you said there were more religions?' asked Daniel when they'd completed the puzzle.

'No,' said Merlin, shaking his beard. 'There's also Islam – a very important religion. People who follow Islam are called Muslims. They believe in one god called Allah. Their holy book is called the Koran.'

'Where do Muslims live?' Daniel wanted to know.

'All over the world,' smiled Merlin. 'But it's the main religion throughout the Middle East and in north Africa.'

'Is that it?' Becky asked. 'Is that all the main religions?'

'No,' said Merlin. 'There's Judaism, which started in Israel about 3,000 years ago. People who follow Judaism are called Jews. They worship in synagogues and their holy book is the Torah, which is written in Hebrew. And there's Sikhism, which is practised in India. Sikhs follow the teachings of Guru Nanak. Many Sikhs don't cut their hair, and the men wear turbans.'

'There's a lot more to learn about all these religions,' Becky said seriously.

'I could write a whole book about them,' Merlin agreed. 'And I still haven't mentioned Confucianism in China, or the Mormon religion, or the special tribal religions followed by millions of people in Africa, Asia, South America and Australia.'

'What sort of religions are they?' asked Daniel.

'All sorts!' said Merlin. 'Some people worship spirits. Others worship nature. Many tribes have a witch-doctor or shaman who organizes the ceremonies and speaks with spirits. And then there are millions of people worldwide who don't believe in a god at all. They're called atheists or humanists. But before we get carried away, I think we'd better have a puzzle!'

Mask Puzzle
Many tribal religions involve the wearing of masks. Masks can be used to make people look like the spirits they worship or to frighten off evil spirits. Here are some masks. Two are exactly the same. Which two?

If you choose . . .	Turn to the world map and cross out . . .
A pair from 1–4	35
A pair from 5–8	14
A pair from 9–12	28

Festivals

Bang! Becky and Daniel jumped as firecrackers began to explode all around them. Through the haze of smoke came a leaping, dancing creature with dozens of legs.

'It's a dragon!' breathed Becky in amazement.

'That's right,' beamed Merlin. 'But don't worry, it's not a *real* dragon. We've come to Hong Kong to celebrate the Chinese New Year.'

'Why do they have so many fireworks?' Daniel shouted above the noise.

'To scare away bad luck,' Merlin explained. 'All over the world people have special ceremonies and festivals at different times of year. In Britain some people welcome the New Year with a custom called first footing. Just after midnight someone knocks at the door carrying a piece of coal. In India people make a pattern on their doorstep using rice flour. What other festivals can you think of?'

'Does Christmas count?' Becky asked.

'Of course,' Merlin nodded. 'In Christian countries Christmas is one of the main festivals. In some countries saints' days are honoured, too. In Sweden, for example, there's a festival to celebrate Saint Lucy, who is the patron saint of sight. Young girls wear crowns surrounded with candles. They attend church services and offer guests special cakes.'

'Are all festivals religious?' Daniel wanted to know.

'Not always,' said Merlin. 'Some of them commemorate famous historical events. There's Thanksgiving, when Americans get together and have a special meal to celebrate the survival of some of the first European settlers. And in India, everyone has a holiday on 2 October to celebrate

78

the birthday of one of India's great leaders, Mahatma Gandhi.'

'I'd like everyone to have a holiday on my birthday,' laughed Daniel.

'I can't arrange that, I'm afraid,' said Merlin. 'But I can arrange a puzzle – and then a trip to the countryside.'

Dragon Puzzle
Here's a Chinese dragon, dancing in the New Year celebrations. There's only one route it can take through the alleyways of Chinatown. Where will it emerge?

If you choose . . .	Turn to the world map and cross out . . .
The fountain	36
The river	21
The park	18

Farming

'Why have we come to the countryside?' asked Becky. They were surrounded by fields full of wheat, or dotted with sheep and cows.

'Because it's in areas like this that most of our food is produced,' explained Merlin. He and the children sat down on a grassy verge. 'Before towns and cities developed, everyone grew their own food. But when they moved into towns, they had to rely on other people to grow it for them.'

'Farmers,' said Daniel. 'They're the people who grow our food.'

'That's right,' nodded Merlin. 'The amount of food a farmer can produce depends on the climate of the country he's living in. Here in Britain we get plenty of rain and sun, and crops grow easily.'

'But if you live in a very hot or cold place, with no rain, or in a desert, you can't grow much,' Becky added.

'Perhaps you can't grow wheat and barley, but there are other crops,' Merlin said. 'In Africa they grow maize, and in India and China rice grows well. Farming methods vary around the world, too. In many countries, particularly the poorest ones, farms are very small and the work is done by hand. In richer countries farms are larger, sometimes thousands of hectares, and farmers use huge machines to help grow and harvest their crops.'

'Do people just farm things to eat?' asked Daniel.

'No, you can farm all kinds of things,' Merlin said. 'For example, you can grow cotton for clothes and rubber trees to produce rubber. You can farm goats and sheep for their wool and produce tobacco for cigarettes. When you've produced these things, you can trade them for the food you need to live.'

'Hey!' cried Becky, 'Look at those animals coming down the track!'

Merlin smiled. 'Here's your next puzzle,' he said. 'And then we'll take a closer look at food.'

Farm Puzzle

On Monday Farmer Giles left his farm gate open and three cows, six pigs, seven hens, a goat, five sheep and two ducks escaped. On Tuesday he managed to round up half the escaped animals. On Wednesday he captured half of those still at large. How many were left to catch on Thursday?

If you choose . . .	Turn to the world map and cross out . . .
6	10
8	20
12	30

Food

After they'd helped round up all his animals, Farmer Giles gave Becky, Daniel and Merlin a lift into the nearby town on his tractor.

'Let's have something to eat,' Merlin suggested, leading the way into a restaurant.

'Great, I'm starving!' said Daniel. They all sat down and looked through the menu. There were lots of things to choose from.

'Those of us who live in the rich Western world can choose from hundreds of different foods every day,' Merlin told the children as they ordered burgers from the waitress. 'But in poorer parts of the world, the choice is much more limited.'

'Doesn't everyone have burgers and chips?' asked Daniel, tucking in.

'Certainly not!' said Merlin huffily. 'Around the world, most people eat very simply. They have a basic, stodgy sort of food which they vary by adding sauces and flavourings.'

'So what do they eat?' asked Becky, dipping her chips in tomato ketchup.

'In Africa they eat maize or millet. They make it into a sort of thick porridge and add spicy pepper sauces and meat. It's delicious,' said Merlin.

'Hmm,' mused Daniel. 'I'll eat almost anything except rice.'

'Then it's a good job you're not Chinese or Indian, because rice is the main food there. In India they serve it with curry and vegetables. In China they have it with vegetables or meat. Sometimes the meat is very unusual – snake meat or ducks' feet.'

Becky and Daniel pulled a face. 'I prefer burgers,' said Daniel.

82

'Time for a food puzzle,' decided Merlin, glancing at his watch. 'And then I think we'll take a look at the kind of houses people live in . . .'

Food Puzzle
The four cheeses in the top row are in order. Which cheese from the bottom row should go next in the sequence?

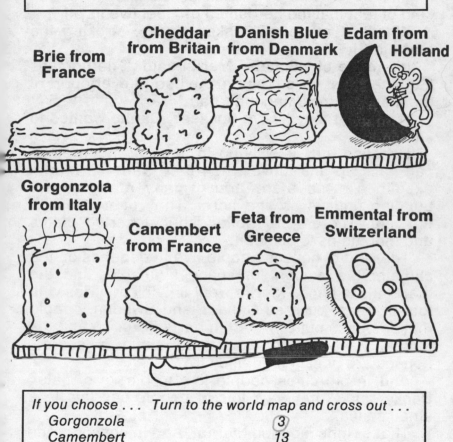

Brie from France

Cheddar from Britain

Danish Blue from Denmark

Edam from Holland

Gorgonzola from Italy

Camembert from France

Feta from Greece

Emmental from Switzerland

If you choose . . .	Turn to the world map and cross out . . .
Gorgonzola	③
Camembert	13
Feta	㉓
Emmental	33

Housing

'Where have you brought us now?' asked Daniel. The three time travellers were sitting in a strange tent made of thick black material. On the floor were brightly coloured wool rugs.

'This is called a yurt,' Merlin told them. 'It's the kind of tent that the herdsmen of Tibet live in.'

'What's it made of?' asked Becky, stroking the black fabric.

'It's made of yak hair,' Merlin said. 'The nomads keep herds of yaks. They make use of every part of the animals, including their hair.'

'Why don't they live in houses?' Daniel wanted to know.

'Because they like living in tents. It means they can pack up and move when they want to,' Merlin explained. 'And there aren't many materials for building houses around here.' They peered out of the tent. There were nothing but deserted plains and mountains to be seen.

'The kind of houses people live in depends on the climate, the amount of space available, and the materials to hand,' Merlin went on. 'In countries with lots of trees, such as Canada and Sweden, people make houses out of wood. In parts of Africa and the Middle East, where wood and stone is scarce, houses are built of mud and straw.'

'And in big cities people live in blocks of flats,' Becky said. 'That way, lots of people can live in a small space.'

'That's right,' nodded Merlin. 'And in hot countries people build their houses to be as cool as possible. They have small windows to keep the sun out. In very dry countries, houses have flat roofs, while in

84

rainy places, roofs tend to be pointed so the water runs off.'

'It all makes sense when you think about it,' mused Daniel.

'Yes,' agreed Merlin. 'On the whole, people *are* very sensible. Let's see how sensible you are when it comes to a housing puzzle!'

Homes Puzzle
See how many different types of home you can find in this wordsearch.

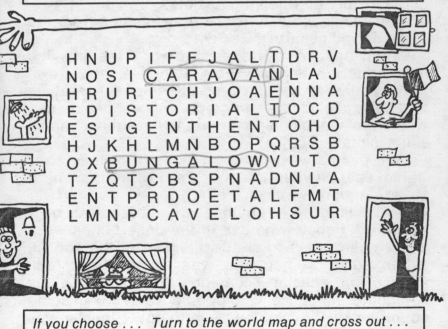

```
H N U P I F F J A L T D R V
N O S I C A R A V A N L A J
H R U R I C H J O A E N N A
E D I S T O R I A L T O C D
E S I G E N T H E N T O H O
H J K H L M N B O P Q R S B
O X B U N G A L O W V U T O
T Z Q T C B S P N A D N L A
E N T P R D O E T A L F M T
L M N P C A V E L O H S U R
```

If you choose . . .	Turn to the world map and cross out . . .
5	16
8	10
10	4
12	39

Clothes

When Merlin and the children came out of the tent, they could see some of the nomads leading their yaks and goats across the pasture. The men wore heavy padded coats and multi-coloured leggings. The women wore brilliant stripy scarves and colourful blouses. Everyone had hats.

'Here in Tibet the temperature goes up and down very quickly,' Merlin explained. 'People wear lots of layers so they can take things off when it gets warm and put more on when it gets cold.'

'And I suppose they make their clothes from the goats' wool,' observed Becky.

Merlin nodded. 'All over the world, people use local materials to make their clothes. Cotton grows in hot countries and it's a good choice for weaving into light, cool clothes. In colder places, people use wool from sheep and goats, or they use the animals' skins to make clothes.'

'And people wear different kinds of clothes, too.' Daniel said. 'If you wore these stripy jackets where I live, everyone would stare.'

Merlin laughed. 'Fashions are different all over the world. People who live in the desert often wear long, loose robes to shade them from the sun. In Japan some women still wear a traditional silk kimono on special occasions. Religious beliefs sometimes influence what people wear, too. In some countries Muslim women have to cover themselves in a black robe and wear a veil or mask if they go out in public.'

'And I like wearing leggings and T-shirts,' giggled Becky.

'If you're such a fashion fan,' said Merlin, 'you should find this puzzle easy! And then we'll finish off our adventure with some sport.'

Hats Puzzle
Match the people and their hats. One hat will be left over. Which one?

If you choose . . .	Turn to the world map and cross out . . .
A	8
B	18
C	15
D	23
E	40

Sports and Games

'Can we go to America and watch a baseball game?' Daniel asked Merlin.

Merlin shrugged. 'Why not?' he asked. There was a flash of green smoke, and the three of them found themselves in the middle of a crowded baseball stadium.

'This is great!' exclaimed Daniel.

'Baseball is one of the great American sports,' Merlin said. 'And Americans also love basketball and American football.'

'Baseball's a bit like rounders. We play that at school,' said Becky.

'That's right!' said Merlin. 'That's how it started. When British people arrived in America they played rounders and, over time, it became baseball. Other countries have their own sports too. In Japan they love sumo wrestling. Two huge wrestlers try to throw each other out of a small circle.'

'I've seen it on TV,' Daniel nodded. 'And Australian football. It's different from football at home.'

'There are lots of other popular sports,' Merlin nodded. 'In Thailand they love kick-boxing. The fighters kick and elbow each other. In Spain and South America they love a sport called pelota. Players throw and catch a ball in a scoop-shaped wicker glove.'

'When we went to France, my dad played boules,' Becky chipped in. 'You roll big balls at a little one and try to hit it.'

'And what about cricket and soccer?' Daniel added. 'I like both of those. And my dad plays golf.'

'All three of those sports were invented in Britain,' Merlin told the children, 'and now they're played all over the world.' He checked his watch. 'Time for another puzzle. Then we'll go back to the cave where we started for a final look at some world facts.'

Good Sports Puzzle
Here are four sportspeople. Can you tell, just from looking at them, which sport they play? We've got five sports listed below. Which sport has no player?

If you choose . . .	Turn to the world map and cross out . . .
Golf	33
Tennis	27
Football	19
Swimming	8
Snooker	10

World Facts

'Must we finish now?' Daniel and Becky asked. Merlin had brought them back to the cave where they'd started their trip through space and time.

'All good things have to come to an end,' Merlin said sadly. He unrolled a map of the world and laid it out on the cave floor. 'But I thought we'd finish with a few world facts. For a start, have you any idea how many people are born every day?'

'A thousand?' ventured Daniel.

'More than that,' smiled Merlin. '270,000 every day – that's almost 200 a minute. Japanese people can expect to live longer than any other people in the world,' he went on. 'On average, women live for 81.9 years and men for 75.8 years.'

'Which country is the richest in the world?' Becky wanted to know.

'That's the USA,' Merlin said. 'Each year the gross national product – the value of all the goods and services the USA produces – works out at around $27,370 per person. The USA also has the most roads in the world, the most daily newspapers, the most TV channels and more dentists and universities than any other country in the world!' By comparison, the "poorest" country in the world is Mozambique in Africa, which has just been torn apart by civil war. There the gross national product averages just $100 per person.'

'Can we have a nice puzzle to finish with?' Becky and Daniel asked.

'I've saved a really good one for last,' Merlin promised.

Birthday Puzzle

Here are all the babies born in a single day at the Hapinapi Maternity Hospital. In the middle of the picture you can see proud Mrs Mumi, who gave birth to some of them. All her babies are identical. How many did she have?

If you choose . . .   Turn to the world map and cross out . . .

If you choose . . .	Turn to the world map and cross out . . .
3	22
4	11
5	13

'It's time for me to go now,' Merlin said when Becky and Daniel had finished the final puzzle. 'But you've still got some work to do, because the search for Ob begins here.'

'What do we have to do now?' Becky asked.

'Look at the map of the world on pages 12–13,' Merlin instructed. 'If there's only one square that hasn't been crossed out, that's the square where you'll find Ob. If you got some of the puzzles wrong, though, you may have more than one untouched square, in which case you'll find some clues on the next few pages. If you look at them closely, you should be able to work out where Ob is.'

Becky and Daniel raised their eyebrows. 'I hope it isn't going to be too tough,' Daniel said.

'Tough enough,' smiled Merlin. 'But you can solve

the last puzzle later – when you get back home. Right now, it's time for you to join your geography class again. They're just going back to the bus.'

'But I don't want to go,' Becky protested. 'You made geography really interesting, Merlin!'

'Yes – you're much more exciting than Mr Harrison,' Daniel added. 'He can't take us into space, or a million years into the past.'

'Well, Mr Harrison isn't a wizard,' said Merlin. 'I really must go now. I've got to give William Shakespeare a spelling lesson. But perhaps we'll meet again.'

'I hope so,' said Becky sadly. As the two children watched, a green mist enveloped Merlin – and suddenly there was a bang and a flash and he disappeared.

'Bye, Merlin,' murmured Daniel. Just then, he and Becky heard Mr Harrison's voice as their group walked back along the beach to the bus.

'Come on,' said Becky, grabbing Daniel's arm. 'Let's catch them up.'

They took one last look at the spot where Merlin had stood, and then they smiled. 'I've got a feeling Merlin will be back before long,' said Daniel.

'I think so too,' agreed Becky.

All About Ob

If you've answered all the puzzles correctly, you'll know which part of the world Ob is in. If you've made some mistakes, you'll probably have several sections of the world map where Ob could be. Use the clues and pieces of information on the following pages to fill in the answers to this mini-questionnaire. A good atlas will help. Your local or school library will have one.

Which country is Ob in? ....

What is the name of the river that flows through Ob? ....

Which ocean does this river flow into? ....

What is the name of the big city with the airport nearest Ob? ....

What is the name of the region in which Ob is situated? ....

What is the name of the famous lake 1,600 km to the east of Ob? ....

If you were visiting Ob in January, would you expect it to be warm or cold?...

What are the industries of the region around Ob? .....
....

WELCOME TO SIBERIA

Siberia stretches from the Ural Mountains to the Pacific Ocean. Much of it is within the Arctic Circle and winters are bitterly cold. Siberia is an area rich in natural resources. It has large areas of forest that supply much of the world's timber. Siberia is also rich in coal, copper, iron, gold, diamonds, oil and natural gas.

The largest city is Novosibirsk, on the River Ob. Novosibirsk is a centre of industry and technology. There are mechanical engineering, textile and food processing industries. Population of around 1,500,000. Just outside the city is Akademgorodok, a big centre of scientific research.

Feeling desperate

If you're really stuck, and you've done all the puzzles and looked at the clues and still can't work out where Ob is, you'll find the answer over the page.

ANSWER

Ob is a town in western Siberia in Russia. It is in the area covered by section 14 of the world map on pages 12–13. The nearest city is Novosibirsk, which is the main city of the region.

The River Ob flows for 3,380 km to the Gulf of Ob in the Arctic Ocean. To look it up, you'll need a large atlas. Ask at your local library or at school for one. Its coordinates are 55.02°N 82.45°E.

Answers

Earth Birth Puzzle

The word LAVA should be in the shaded box.

Human Puzzle

There are ten differences.

Jigsaw Puzzle

The answer is South America.

Fossil Puzzle

The dinosaur was a pterodactyl.

Hot Spot Puzzle

There are four people hidden at the oasis.

Rainforest Puzzle

The answer is 9. The words are: piranha, scorpion, monkey, parrot, spider, cactus, camel, sloth, frog. There's also a penguin hidden away, but penguins prefer cold places!

Iceberg Puzzle

Iceberg 4 is the correct answer.

Coal-mining Puzzle

Ned's route is the shortest.

Ocean Puzzle

The correct sequence is: Indian, Atlantic, Pacific. The Mediterranean is not an ocean, but a sea!

Underwater Puzzle

There are six pairs in the picture.

Strange Seas Puzzle

The answer is the River Lark.

Coastline Puzzle

The answer is Perrin Harbour.

Port Puzzle

The answer is 5.

Mountain Puzzle

The answer is A.

Earthquake Puzzle

Los Mycat is the city hit by the quake.

Cloud Puzzle

The lowest layer of cloud is nimbostratus.

Auntie Madge's Puzzle

The time in Brisbane is 4 a.m. which is *not* a good time for Christy to phone Auntie Madge!

Earth Lines Puzzle

The correct answer is 0°, 0°.

Map-making Puzzle

The most accurate map is C.

Map-reading Puzzle

Kell is village A.

Swashbuckling Puzzle

There are five things out of place in the picture.

Human Race Puzzle

The answer is 13.

House-building Puzzle

The answer is eight friends.

Town Puzzle
The answer is B.

Lost Cities Puzzle
A matches both plans.

Flag Puzzle
The odd one out is 4. It is the flag of the European Community.

Sightseeing Puzzle
Italy is the odd one out. St Paul's Cathedral is in London, England.

Language Puzzle
Kangaroo is the Australian aboriginal word meaning 'I don't know'.

Writing Puzzle
The treasure is hidden behind the mask.

Money Puzzle
Wallet C gives you the most spending power.

Religions Puzzle
The answer is B.

Mask Puzzle

Masks 2 and 3 are the same.

Dragon Puzzle

The route leads to the fountain.

Farm Puzzle

There are six animals still at large.

Food Puzzle

The answer is Feta. The cheeses are in alphabetical order.

Homes Puzzle

There are ten different types of home: caravan, boat, hut, flat, house, bungalow, cave, hotel, ranch and tent.

Hats Puzzle

The odd hat out is B.

Good Sports Puzzle

The odd sport out is football.

Birthday Puzzle

Mrs Mumi has five babies, known as quins.

THE ALIENS ARE COMING
Phil Gates

The greenhouse effect is warming up the earth so that snowmen could become an endangered species. It also means you may have to eat more ice-cream to keep cool in summer. But worse, it may cause the spread of alien plants which will cause havoc in the countryside and could cause some native plants, which like a cool moist climate, to become extinct.

Find out for yourself, through the experiments and information in this original and entertaining book, just what is happening now and what is likely to happen in the future.

Become a scientist and help warn the world about the dangers ahead!

LAND AHOY! THE STORY OF
CHRISTOPHER COLUMBUS
Scoular Anderson

The colour of the sea was probably the last thing that Christopher Columbus was thinking about when he set off, five hundred years ago, on one of the greatest voyages of discovery ever made. His journey was just as adventurous and just as important as the first space flight to the moon was this century. But Columbus set sail into the vast ocean not really knowing where he was going or, once he had got there, what he'd found!

Now you can be an explorer by reading this book and finding out just what an extraordinary man Columbus was – how he managed to travel the world and put America on the map for the first time.